ANGUS MACGREGOR

Hart Mountain Hotshots, Book 3

Drive My Engine, *Rookie*

Gay Firemen Erotica

About the Publisher

4Fun Publishing, a member of **BLVNP Incorporated**, 340 S. Lemon #6200, Walnut CA 91789, info@blvnp.com / legal@blvnp.com
NOTE: Due to the highly emotional reaction of some people to works of erotic fiction, any email sent to the above address that contains foul language or religious references is automatically deleted by our anti-spam software and will not be seen. All other communications are welcome.

DISCLAIMER

Please don't be stupid and kill yourself. This book is a work of FICTION. Do not try any new sexual practice that you find in this book. It is fiction and not to be confused with reality. Neither the author nor the publisher or its associates assume any responsibility for any loss, injury, death or legal consequences resulting from acting on the contents in this book. Every character in this book is over 18 years of age. The author's opinions are not to be construed as the opinions of the publisher. The material in this book is for entertainment purposes ONLY. Enjoy.

Hart Mountain Hotshots, Book 3

Drive My Engine, Rookie

Gay Firemen Erotica

By: Angus MacGregor

JESSE AND Brandon woke up early once the morning noises of the fire camp began to get loud. It took less than a minute for them to maneuver around into a hungry early morning sixty-nine with a thick protein shake reward at the end for them both. Brandon continued to fondle Jesse's penis and scrotum as he looked for some new underwear to put on. He just enjoyed the sensation of being able to touch his friend like this with no worries or restraint.

Jesse pulled on some new briefs and fished for some new socks. Brandon found his own clothes and began to get dressed.

"Bet you need to piss again," Jesse said.

"Yep, like a Russian race horse," Brandon added.

"Why is it a Russian race horse?" Jesse asked, bewildered.

"I don't know. My dad used to always say that."

They crawled out of the tent and laced up their boots and grabbed their gear for the day. They saw Colton and Ben grabbing things out of their tent and smiled, thinking of last night. Brandon just remembered and grabbed Jesse's arm.

"Hold on, dude. I want to check something."

He walked over to the tent on the other side of theirs and peeked inside. Tom was long gone it seemed but Ian was still sawing logs. His big naked ass was showing, sleeping bag discarded to the side. Around his hole, matted hair was plastered against his skin. The dark pink hole was winking in the morning light.

"That is a well-used man pussy if I ever saw one," Jesse said in his low, early morning growl. Brandon snickered in agreement.

Jesse reached a hand into the tent and gripped one of Ian's feet and shook it. The boy's toes and arch were covered with a fine down of blond curls much like Jesse's. Ian turned over and exposed a rock hard morning erection that was pointing to the top of the tent in a dramatic salute. His thick blond bush framed a six and a half inch circumcised penis that was thick and wide, his nutsack hanging low in the warmth of the tent interior.

"Shit, he looks like a smaller version of you," Brandon said, starting to reach out and grip Ian's shaft.

"Damn, Bran - you have no restraint at all, kid," Jesse laughed. "Hey, Ian, wake up brother, you are gonna be late," Jesse said loudly.

Ian opened bleary eyes and sat up a bit, registering who was talking to him. "It's too early," he groaned, lying back down.

Jesse looked at Brandon. "OK, now might be a good time for you to do your inappropriate touching thing."

Brandon smiled and reached out, gripping Ian's full sack and giving his testicles a hard squeeze. Ian howled and rolled into the fetal position.

"Stop it you dick," he cried, holding his sack.

"Get up, you idiot," Jesse commanded. "You don't want to be late today. Come on and move your big ass."

Ian sat up and realized then he was bare-ass naked. Brandon saw his face flush crimson but he just crawled to his duffle and began looking for his clothes. Brandon took off for the can to relieve his full bladder. Jesse hung back, enjoying watching Ian bent over looking for his clothes, thinking to himself, now that is a fuckable ass. Finally he spoke.

"How's your cornhole, buddy?"

Ian's head spun around and he stared at Jesse. He grabbed his boxers and struggled to pull them up.

"It's fine. Why would you ask that?"

"Just sounded like Old Tom was plowing you pretty good in there last night." Then in a whispered voice he said, "Oh Jesus, Mary, and Joseph it's too big to fit--oh Christ, oh my fucking God, don't stop...!"

"Shut the fuck up," Ian hissed with a snarl. "You don't know what you are..."

"Maybe not, but I know the sound of butt fucking. And you sir, have the glow of a freshly plucked cherry."

Ian finished getting dressed and moved to climb out of the tent and stepped into his boots. He looked around as if wondering if others were listening in. "Don't tell anyone, okay? Please."

Jess draped his heavy arm around Ian's shoulders. "No worries, bud. I got your back. Hope it was as fun as it sounded. "

Ian grinned. "You have no idea. Who would have never guessed the old guy could make it feel so good."

"That cock ring must do the trick, huh?"

"He was fucking huge."

The guys began walking to the chow hall. The morning was cool and mist hung in the hills that surrounded the camp. Ian gripped Jesse's arm and pulled him to a stop.

"You really won't tell, right? I'm not gay. I just, I don't know. I never did anything like that before. It was not what I expected."

"In a good way or a bad way?"

"A little too good, I think. And by the way, Tom and I heard you boys last night too. Sounded like my cornhole wasn't the only one getting a workout."

"I have no idea what you are talking about," Jesse answered with sanctimonious aloofness.

"Yeah, right," Ian said with obvious sarcasm.

He and Jesse grabbed their breakfast and found Brandon sitting with Aaron, Nick, and Jordan. The five of them made up the rookie class of the Hotshots. Chad, Bayard, Ben, Colton, Sam and Eric were the veteran firefighters along with six others the rookies had yet to meet. Tom and Rick were assistant crew boss leaders and Jake was the top dog.

"Did you ladies get your tampons all pushed in and everything?" Aaron teased. The short, stocky guy smiled widely with his mouth full of breakfast, his red-brown beard framing his big, pearly smile.

"Actually we just finished up feeding our cocks to your sister and she says 'hi,'" Jesse said with deadpan finality.

"Yeah well your dad blew me and said it was great."

The table exploded with laughter. "That is the stupidest thing you have ever said," Nick added with a howl.

"Shut up," Aaron retorted, defeated.

Jesse sat down between Brandon and Ian and started in on his biscuits and gravy. He felt Brandon slide his hand down and grip his knee and then up to his thigh. Jesse rested his hand on Brandon's and squeezed. It was weird, Jesse thought. All that touching and kissing and fucking last night and this casual, hidden touch of his buddy's hand under the table was more electric and sensual than anything else.

He held on to Brandon's hand until he finished his breakfast. He gave it a hard squeeze and let it go, enjoying the slight blush to the cheeks of Brandon's face. Jesse noticed Ian on his right. He spread his legs out wider and felt his right leg rest against Ian's. Ian moved his leg away momentarily, but then he cut his eyes over to Jesse and let his leg lightly touch the big blond firefighter again. Jesse pressed his leg against it and slid his hand over to grip Ian's knee. Jesse slowly slid his hand all the way up to Ian's crotch until it rested against his big ballsack. Ian didn't move other than to spread his legs wider and let Jesse fondle him discretely while continuing to drink his coffee and chat with the other guys. Jesse's fingers traced the outline of Ian's mushroom head, feeling him flex his member against his touch.

Jesse's cell phone rang, which broke him away from his crotch exploration. He looked at the screen and saw it was Parker. A pang of panic and guilt swept over him. He was supposed to have called. He swiped his finger over the screen and answered.

"Hey P, how's it going? How's Palo Alto?"

"Good, Jess. Hey how's fire school?

"So far pretty good. The crew is great. Cool guys and all that."

"Cool."

Jesse wondered if it was just him or was this the dumbest conversation ever? He kept racking his brain for something interesting to say, but all he could think of was his tongue sliding into Brandon's mouth or in his ass. He thought of his cock disappearing into that curly little hobbit's bunghole, leaving his seed behind. He and Parker were going to do that. They had talked about waiting until he came home on his break before the fall term and they were going to take each other's virginity. They were going to fuck and fuck and fuck until their nuts were empty. Now all he could think about was Brandon's dick in his ass and how fucking amazing that felt.

"So how are the classes going?"

"Good. Hard. Man, these fuckers down here are so smart. I am already studying all the time."

"I bet. My stuff's a lot easier," Jesse said. *Christ, how lame is this phone call*, he thought. "Um, so how's your roommate?"

The line went quiet for almost twenty seconds. Jesse thought for a moment he had lost the call and was almost glad about it. Then Parker came back on the line.

"Um, he's good. You know, cool. Shane's on the football team. Defense guy. Big moose like you," he said with a laugh. Then he added, "Um, you would like him. He's not a dick or anything."

"Oooh, I don't know. I'm a Duck fan, buddy. Those damn Trees, that football team is good."

"Yeah, I know."

More silence. Jesse finally broke in and said, "Is everything okay, man?"

"I kind of fucked up, Jess."

Jesse swallowed and felt his bunghole contract. What the hell is this about? He already was feeling so guilty. For fuck's sake, he was feeling up Ian just a few minutes ago like a total man whore.

"What happened?"

"I kind of…oh Christ, I didn't mean for it to…Fuck!"

Jesse gripped the phone and walked farther away from a group of crews walking near the parking lot. "What the hell, just tell me, dude."

"Shane's been fucking me. He's been fucking me and I have loved it. I know we said we were going to do it together first and I love you man, and you mean the world to me but…Oh God, it just happened. His dick is just so, oh fuck, I am sorry, brother. I feel like I am the shittiest friend in the whole world."

Jesse realized he was still holding his breath. He had not expected this. He was the rat, he was the shitty friend. Parker was away from home and trying to do something new. Jesse had seen some of those Stanford football players. No doubt, he would be pretty happy to let someone like Andrew Luck slide his big cock into his hole. Holy shit, he was getting hard just thinking about that.

"Parker. Listen to me," Jesse started. It sounded like Parker was sniffing, maybe like he was crying or something. "I know we planned to stick together and bone each other our first time and all that. But brother, you are there and I am here and I know you must have felt real bad about hooking up with your roomie, but I bet he is a good guy. I bet he is smoking hot and hell, if one of those big Duck linemen was walking around my room *nekkid* all the time, I bet I would be wanting him to tap my ass as well."

"I really am sorry. I didn't plan it. We just spend a lot of time together and you are right. He is hot and does walk around naked sometimes. He…um, was a virgin too."

"Did you fuck him back?" Jesse asked, more annoyed and angry than he would have expected.

"No. He says he doesn't think he would like that."

"Are you okay with that?"

"I don't know. For now it's ok. I really like it, Jess. Wait until you try it. I think you will love it."

For a split second, Jesse started to say, Hey you ass hat, I have been fucking a guy and he fucked me and I just might be crazy about him. But instead he said, "Yeah, I know. Hey buddy. It's all cool. I'm not mad or anything. I hope you have a great term with Shane. I gotta run to this next training. Will talk soon."

Jesse stood still for over two minutes just letting conversation percolate in his head. He thought of Parker, all the fun times they shared. That first amazing night in Seattle and the rest of the school term and early summer. They had swallowed a gallon of sperm from each other over the weeks. But for some reason, they had never taken the plunge and fucked. They talked about it, flirted about it, shared stories about what their experiences had been like with their girlfriends. But they had had more than a dozen chances to do the deed, including that weekend they had spent together at Parker's house. They had been alone for three days. They ended up staying naked almost the entire time. Jesse lost count of how many times they had sucked each other off. But even though they slept naked together every night, they never slid inside one another and really didn't kiss either.

Contrast that with one night with Brandon, Jesse thought. In that cramped tent, he had fucked his first ass, kissed and made out, eaten a furry butt hole, swallowed nut, and to top it all off, lost his own ass cherry to his new buddy. He had to admit, getting topped by Brandon felt way better than he had imagined it would and he loved the way both of them took turns pleasuring each other. Jesse had never been someone's boyfriend, not really. There had been a half-dozen girls that he had been friendly with. He went on plenty of dates and made sure when he took a girl to prom that the night ended up with his dick being sucked (badly) and a quick fuck with a rubber. But he had never cared about any of them other than being friendly. The sex was just a means to an end: he wanted to cum and was bored with only jacking off. He liked sucking on their tits and the inside of their pussy was tight and wet, but he didn't like their clingy neediness. He hated the pointless phone calls demanding he talk about his feelings. And he despised how the girls demanded he give them all his attention, with nothing left of his time for his friends. Bros before Hoes, he really understood what that meant now.

Jesse wandered in to the boy's bathroom, the one on the other side of the lunch room, and ducked in for a quick shit before he got busy for the day. Oddly, for some reason the stalls had the doors still on them in this bathroom, which was luxurious compared to taking a dump with everyone watching you like the other bathrooms. From the looks of it, another firefighter had the same idea and had taken the middle stall. Jesse went to the last stall and locked the door.

The air was raunchy with piss and shit smells, but it was clean and there was toilet paper, so Jesse unfastened his pants and slid them down to his ankles, pushed his dick down between his big legs and sat on the john. As he released his bowels, Jesse noticed a movement on his left. He turned his head and saw there was a hole in the wall. He could see into the next stall and the firefighter there. He saw brown furry legs and a bright red t shirt, probably a crew member from Eagle Point Hotshots, an all Latino crew. He could also see the firefighter had his penis out and was stroking it as he sat there. The other guy stood and slid his big brown uncut cock through the hole. The foreskin was slid back and the dark pink tip was glistening with precum.

"Hola amigo, mi polla carrera para mí," the faceless firefighter whispered through the stall.

Jesse's high school Spanish kicked in and he gripped the thick, young penis and began to slide his hand back and forth, watching the pink head disappear behind the foreskin and then reappear. Jesse looked up and saw the young man's hands gripping the top of the wall as he pushed his cock through the hole, Jesse masturbating him with haste.

"Oh Dios, chuparme la polla mi amigo," the Mexican crew member said breathlessly.

Jesse slid forward on the pot and wrapped his lips around the fat cock. The guy on the other side moaned and continued to piston his cock out of Jesse's warm mouth. The brown penis tasted of soap and piss and musky sweat. Jesse reached up and placed his hand over the firefighter's hand gripping the wall, their fingers entwining. So much precum was leaking out of the guy's cock, the member was slick with spit and cock honey. Jesse felt the young man's dick head swell in his mouth.

"O Fuck, amigo, estoy llegando!"

He pulled off a split second before the thick tan burrito erupted thick white semen across his lips and chin whiskers. Jesse suddenly realized he had been stroking his own cock this entire time. With cum dripping off his face to his shirt, Jesse stood up and shoved his penis through the hole. He felt the warm hand of the firefighter stroke his shaft and then a hot wet mouth slide over it, sucking long and deep. Jesse face fucked the guy through the hole, banging his balls against the wall.

"Jesus, buddy I'm going to cum!"

Jesse unloaded his nuts into the mouth of the guy, who hungrily gulped and swallowed the thick load, milking the last drop free. Jesse thought his knees would buckle as the guy sucked and sucked his cock until Jesse had to pull free of the hungry mouth. Jesse pulled up his pants and opened the door of his stall just as the door of the middle stall opened. The stocky firefighter in the red shirt turned around with a big grin on his face. Jesse looked around and reached out and grabbed the young guy's hand.

"Gracias a amigo por chupar mi polla tan bien."

The firefighter grinned wider and pushed Jesse back inside his stall, pressing him against the wall. He pushed Jesse's pants and underwear down under his balls and gripped his junk while planting an unexpected open-mouth kiss. Jesse could taste his semen on the guy's breath as his tongue slipped inside.

"I liked the way you sucked my dick too, amigo," the firefighter said, squeezing Jesse's balls and dick again. "Chad Maldanado on your crew, I grew up with him. He taught me how to suck a cock." He gave Jesse one last quick kiss and gripped his meaty ass in one hand. "Next time, I'll fuck your pussy, Miho, and make you my bitch." Then as he was walking away he turned around and gripped his junk "And maybe that little hobbit amigo of yours too."

Jesse closed the stall door and locked it again. He slid his pants down and sat back down on the toilet. He unrolled some paper and cleaned off his face. Unrolled a bit more and cleaned his ass. What the fuck just happened, he thought to himself. Jesse started to get up when another big pair of boots walked into the bathroom and to the middle stall. Jesse sat still hoping this guy would be quick so he could make an escape. The guy stood in front of the toilet and pissed loudly into the bowl. The guy was standing back far enough so that Jesse could see the round ass and heavy balls pulled out, along with a shockingly thick penis, round head wide and flared. He tugged on his shaft and flicked the last couple of drops off then turned and slid his cock into the hole.

"Get busy, Rookie," the low whisper spoke.

Like a hypnosis victim, Jesse took the fat cock into his mouth and began to suck. The man pumped rhythmically into his mouth, oozing precum and drops of piss. The man pulled his dick out of the hole, leaving Jesse on his knees wondering what was going on. Then the boots shuffled, pants were pushed down to the floor and the man slid his knees and naked groin under the wall, penis fully erect. Jesse reached back and gripped the man's ass and with his other hand gripped his balls and swallowed the cock down to the short, cropped brown pubes. This was a beautiful penis, Jesse had to admit. Perfect proportions, balls big and round in a loose floppy sack. Jesse sucked and sucked and bathed those balls as the man leaned back and fucked in and out of his mouth.

"Cumming," the husky voice said from the other stall.

Jesse felt the sour blast of sperm hit the back of his throat with four large loads. He sucked and licked the beautiful penis until it was clean and wet, still rock hard. As the man pulled back and began to pull up his pants, his eye peeked through the hole and straight at Jesse. The eye, pale ice blue, crinkled in a smile.

"Holy shit, Rookie. I knew you were your Dad's boy, but didn't know you had those quality cocksucking skills too. Next time, I want that big dick of yours up my ass and I promise to return the favor too." The man turned to leave. Again, Jesse unlocked the door and stepped out.

Eric turned around and grinned. "By the way. You are fucking late, rookie," he said, making his way out the door.

Jesse checked his watch.

"Fuck!" he swore. Flushing the crapper and buckling his belt, he ran out of the stall and right into Rick who had come in the bathroom looking for him.

"Let's go, Rookie," Rick bellowed. "What's your hold up? You can jack off on your own time." Then he looked at Jesse's chin and added, "You must be quite the shooter. Looks like you launched your nut all the way on your face."

Jesse's face went scarlet as he quickly wiped his chin, following Rick out of the john. He and the crew were going to be working on S-215 in the morning with more classroom study and then in the afternoon, they would be doing driving training in the engines. He rushed into the classroom and flopped into the chair between Brandon and Ian.

"Where the hell have you been?" Brandon asked quietly as the instructor began the class. He leaned over and inhaled. "Jesus, you smell like a used rubber. You better bathe tonight, kiddo, if you want to bone me again."

"Just shut up," Jesse hissed back.

As the instructor lead the class, Jesse kept thinking about his morning. First there was that crazy phone call confessional with Parker. Then the glory hole swap with the Mexican guy and learning Chad had taught the guy how to suck dick. And if that wasn't enough, old blue eyes Eric had fed him his perfect cock and dropped that little tidbit about him being as good a cocksucker as his dad? WTF!

Brandon leaned over again, his hand sliding onto Jesse's thigh. "Dude, you know I will let you copy my paper but you should at least try to listen."

"Eat me, Frodo," Jesse snapped in a voice louder than it needed to be. Ian laughed along with several others. Brandon's face flushed and he turned away from Jesse.

The instructor finished the class and passed out the exam papers. Brandon got busy and ripped through the questions in no time, long before Jesse had a chance to really look at what the answers were. Brandon got up and laid his paper on the instructor's desk and headed to the bathroom. Jesse sat there looking at the test paper, not knowing any of the answers at all. He started to get up when he felt Ian's arm press against his, giving him a clear view of his answers. Jesse looked at him with gratitude and contrition and he quickly scribbled down the answers. Ian went up and turned in his paper and about half a minute later, Jesse followed him out of the room. He caught up with the blond boy in the hall.

"Thanks for saving my ass, Ian," Jesse said sincerely.

"No worries dude, but that was seriously not cool with Brandon. That kid really looks up to you and that was pretty shitty."

"I know. I'm going to try and fix it," Jesse said with resolution.

Sometime after lunch, with a lot of talking and apologizing, Brandon finally accepted Jesse's apology and told him to forget it.

"You are a dumb shit for sure, but it's okay. What the hell got into you? Have you been a man whore like this for a long time?" Brandon said with a laugh. The guys had walked past their tent into the wooded area beside it to have some privacy.

Jesse shook his head. "Man, I don't know how that all happened. I swear to God I have never just sucked some guy before or anything like that. You were the second guy I ever sucked. I think it was just the surprise of it and that shit with Parker and everything."

"So were you and Parker like boyfriends or something?"

"No, not really. Just longtime friends that found out we liked dick together. We kind of always thought we might keep on fooling around," Jesse said then added, "Guess we kind of thought we would end up together or at least would pop each other's ass cherry."

"That delightful experience got to be mine instead," Brandon said smiling. "And you plucked my grape good yourself, buddy." The small guy slid beside Jesse and felt Jesse cradle his curly head in his arm and bend down and kiss him on the head.

"Frodo, huh?" Brandon said leaning against Jesse, feeling the familiar stir in his groin.

"One of my favorite movies. He and that Sam must have fooled around some, don't you think?"

"So you're Samwise huh? Well for God's sake don't cry all the time like him, okay?"

"Only when you're boning me," Jesse laughed. "What time is it? I don't want to be late again."

"We've got another twenty minutes or so," Brandon said. "So tell me more about your whoring in the bathroom."

Jesse recounted the blow jobs, the big Mexican burrito, the juicy tidbit about Chad and then Eric's blue eyes and perfect cock and the revelation that somehow his dad had either been a cocksucker or at least enjoy getting blown himself.

"That is crazy, man. I would freak if I found out my old man liked dick, though it might be kind of sexy too. I wish I had seen you sucking that big brown boner. How was the uncut thing?"

"Fine. His dick was nice and clean. If he had been digging fire line all day or hadn't bathed in a few, it might be nasty."

"And Eric. Shit man, he's a married guy, right?"

"Yeah. He's the one with those triplets, remember?"

"That's right. Man, he must have some top quality jizz to make triplets."

"Well, it sure tasted good. It was fucking amazing. That dick is perfect. Hey, we better get going."

"Okay, thanks. Now I'm hard."

The guys made it back to the parking lot and found the engine they would be training in. Soon, Rick and Bayard joined them along with Ian of all things. The veteran firefighters began to take the rookies through the safety checks and instructed them on the use of the equipment on board. The veteran crew members quizzed the rookies on hand tools, safety precautions, pump operation, use of personal protective equipment, and engine operation. They explained each of the gauges and read-outs and made sure they understood the basics of operation.

The guys' heads were full when the vets told them to load up in the back seat. Rick climbed into the front along with Bayard and they took off toward Rock Creek road and into the forest. Rick demonstrated how to downshift or apply the air brakes in the right way. He took the guys around sharp curves, off-road in areas where they might roll and pump for firefighting, and even some regular highway driving. After 45 minutes or so, he stopped on a landing far out of town that overlooked a verdant ocean of Douglas Fir. Rick and Bayard pointed out various landmarks to the guys and identified different forest structures and habitats.

While showing the sights, Rick pulled out his big cock and let a clear yellow fountain of piss rain down on some sword ferns down below him. Bayard unzipped and pulled out his uncut penis too, sliding the thick skin back and adding his stream to Rick's. The rookies smiled and shrugged their shoulders and unzipped and joined in the water show, sending big loud piss streams into the ferns. Jesse and the other rookies stood with their hands on their hips, watching the golden arches spatter the ground and vegetation, enjoying the warm air caressing their cocks like a velvet glove.

Jesse shook his head and smiled. What was it about group outdoor urination that was fucking hot every time? He felt his penis swell and noticed his wasn't the only one. All three rookies were more or less at attention by the time they finished.

Rick told Bayard to grab the canteens off the truck while he continued discussing the surrounding land area with the rookies and knocking the last drips of pee off his cock. Bayard came back with four canteens he had pulled out of the guy's fire packs and handed them around. It was fairly warm and the guys were parched, so the rookies took big long gulps of water.

"Hey Rookie, found this in your pack too. You want to show us how this thing works?" Bayard said with a sly grin, holding up the Fleshlight.

Brandon spewed water out of his mouth and nose, shocked and mortified by the sex toy being held aloft in Bayard's big, thick fingers.

Rick roared in laughter. Jesse and Ian looked dumbfounded. Bayard looked into the toy like it was a telescope, sliding a finger scandalously inside the foam lips of the Fleshlight.

"Ho, Jeezuz, I bet that feels good on your pecker," he said. "You like pounding your pud with this thing, huh Frodo?"

Brandon's lips were set in a hard line. It was nice to see that name was already making the rounds. He reached for the toy but Bayard held it just out of his reach.

"Hold on. I ought to at least get to give it a try. Maybe you can show me how it works."

"I figured even your limited intelligence could figure that one out," Brandon said with a snap. Jesse winced when he heard his friend insult the veteran firefighter. This wasn't going to be so good, he thought.

"Hey, none of that, Hobbit boy," Bayard said moving over to Brandon. "Play nice and you are gonna do fine here. Now, slide this thing on my boner and show me how it works."

With that, Bayard pushed his pants down to his knees and gripped his dick again. His penis was already almost hard, the tip shining wet, his foreskin pulled back. He handed the toy to Brandon, who turned to Jesse and Ian, looking for some way out of this mortification. Finally he just rolled his eyes, stepped up and slid the Fleshlight slowly down the shaft of Bayard's penis.

"Ho-lee shit," Bayard hissed. "That feels amazing. Oh Jeez, it's like already full of something. Christ, I bet it's your rookie baby gravy. Oh man, that is gnarly, sliding around in your used rubber."

Brandon's face was bright red as he continued to pump the toy back and forth on Bayard's boner, the slurping sounds of the Fleshlight sounding scandalously loud and obscene. The onlookers continued to move in closer, making a ring of observers surround Brandon and Bayard.

Brandon could feel his cock betray him and fill with blood, causing an obvious erection straining against his fire pants and he had to wonder why it appeared there was so much jizz in that damn toy. He looked around and noticed the clear outline of Ian's and Jesse's dicks pressing against their own pants. He looked over at Rick, who was visibly adjusting his monster meat as well.

Bayard was slumped against the side of the engine, eyes closed. The man's large egg-sized testicles rose and fell in a furry sack as the toy continued to pound back against him. He had Brandon's head held close to his, their noses practically touching. Jesse watched as Bayard's hand reached behind and gripped Brandon's ass in one big meaty mitt, digging his fingers deep into the rookie's ass crack.

Rick stepped up and pulled the toy and Brandon's hand away from Bayard's cock that sprang free and thumped against his yellow Nomex shirt, all eight inches of it, slick and wet.

"What the fuck, man," Bayard said, obviously annoyed. "I was getting ready to blow my wad."

Rick pushed his own pants down and his even larger penis flopped free. Brandon went ahead and guided the Fleshlight to his dark pink, flared dick head. It looked for a moment that the head wasn't going to fit into the foam lips. Then the monster parted the lips and slid inside and Rick sighed loudly.

"Motherfucker, that's nice," Rick whispered as Brandon pumped the toy back and forth on his member. Rick's large balls rolled and bounced in his thick thatched scrotum, carpeted with red fur. The forest officer pumped in and out of the toy a few more times and then pulled off, his near nine-inch penis wet and glistening in the midday sun, a long trail of cock snot dangling from the dangerous tip. His hand darted out and he grabbed Ian by the shirt and pulled the startled boy toward him. Ian tripped and fell to his knees in front of Rick's massive erection. Rick grabbed the back of Ian's head and pulled it toward his penis.

"Go ahead and clean me up, Rookie," Rick said with authority. Ian's eyes were wide but he didn't hesitate. He obediently opened his mouth and felt the slick head of Rick's cock slide inside. Rick pressed forward until he was buried balls deep in Ian's mouth, full bush framing the boy's watering eyes. He held Ian's head there until he began to gag and then pulled off, the firefighter choking and coughing. He gripped the boy on either side of his head and began to stroke his cock in and out of his mouth, his big balls banging against Ian's chin, lines of spit and slobber running out of the corners of his mouth. Rick pulled his cock out and began to slap it against the rookie's face until it was wet and coated with precum and spit. Rick pulled Ian up and planted a big, hungry kiss on the rookie's open mouth, exploring it with his thick tongue, his red goatee rubbing hard against the blond boy's smooth face.

"Shit, kid. I like you. You can be the first to drive the engine."

"Thanks," Ian said wiping his face with a sleeve and opening the door of the cab, preparing to climb up inside.

"Hold it there, buddy. Lose the pants first," Rick said flatly.

"Huh?"

"No pants, Rook. You gotta earn the right to have them back. Strip down, no pants or shorts. Put your boots back on and get in there bareass. That's the rules."

Stunned, Ian began to slowly unfasten his belt. Jesse and Brandon turned to each other and began to chuckle. Bayard stepped up between them.

"What's so funny, dickweeds?"

"Um, nothing," both said, holding back smiles.

Bayard continued. "You idiots don't seem to get it. You heard Rick. Strip down to your boots. And climb in the back. You sit there bareassed until it's your turn to drive. And since you think it's so funny, Rick and I will give you a special treat while you wait to drive. So get *nekkid*, Scrotes." And with that, Bayard crawled into the back seat of the engine with Rick jumping into the passenger side of the front.

Jesse and Brandon shook their heads and began to unfasten their boot laces and tug them off before pulling off their pants and underwear. Brandon kept thinking this was insane, standing bare ass naked on a remote landing in a shirt and boots. The wind had picked up and was tickling the fuzzy curly hairs on his tight sack. He looked over and saw Ian's pink butt disappear up into the engine cab. Jesse joined beside him naked from the waist down, his fat cock poking ridiculously out from beneath his fire shirt. The rookies gathered up their gear and stowed it in one of the engine boxes on the back of the truck and climbed into the truck, Jesse heading for the front to sit with Rick and Brandon beside Bayard.

The first thing Jesse noticed when he grabbed the handle to pull himself up into the engine was the fact that Rick's fire pants were bunched around his ankles, leaving his legs and groin naked. The man's thick penis was still erect, a large drop of precum oozing from the large slit in the flared mushroom head. Jesse looked in the back and saw Bayard's pants were down to his ankles as well.

"Got a good seat for you boys right here," Bayard said patting his lap and erection. Jesse noticed he was holding a big bottle of lube. "But first things first: get down and start sucking, Frodo."

"You too, Rookie. Let's see if you truly are your father's son 'cause he could suck the chrome off a bumper," Rick said, sliding one boot out of his pants and spreading his legs wide so Jesse could crawl between.

Jesse was so stunned by the whole situation that the shocking reference to his dad didn't even register. He looked back and saw Brandon's curly head already hard at work on Bayard's boner. Bayard's hand traced the line of fuzz in Brandon's ass crack. Bayard opened the bottle of lube and let a big stream flow down the small guy's crack and he massaged it into his hole. Jesse felt Rick's big hand on top of his head guiding his buzz cut down on that giant prick. Jesse opened his mouth wide and felt it fill by the time the head and a small bit of the shaft slid inside. His eyes bulged and watered as Rick continued to push his head down further on the massive shaft. Jesse gripped the bull balls and began to suck in earnest, thinking to himself, *this is crazy, but fuck, this cock is the best thing I have ever sucked.* After laboring with sucking as much of Rick's penis as he could, he pulled off and began to bathe the big nuts with his tongue, fitting one at a time into his mouth. Jesse looked up and Ian was staring at him, eyes wide with wonder, his own cock hard and leaking by this time.

"OK, Rook, let's see if you can keep from killing all of us. Go through the safety checks and head out," Rick said while he gripped his shaft and fed it to Jesse once again. He grabbed the lube from Bayard and tipped it so a large stream flowed into the blond furry ass crack of the rookie. Jesse moaned as Rick's thick finger penetrated his anus and began to finger fuck him.

Ian moved the engine down the road and worked his ways through the gears smoothly, only popping the clutch once as he got up to a decent speed. Jesse looked up and Brandon was hanging over the front seat, his ass pressed tight against Bayard's bearded face. Bayard licked and slurped on the rookie's hole, probing his furry ass ring with his tongue. Rick pulled Jesse up and maneuvered the big boy around straddling his lap, so he was gripping the dashboard. Rick's mouth began to suck Jesse's hole until it was wet and sopping.

"OK, Ian, take the next road on your left. You will need to shift into low once you get on it," Rick commanded. He gripped Jesse's waist with his big hands and positioned the rookie's asshole above his erection. Jesse felt the large head press against his sphincter.

"Oh goddamn."

Jesse heard Brandon bark from the backseat as Bayard penetrated his pussy. Jesse felt his own ass ring open and then tighten down on Rick's giant member. The man held in one place as the quivering muscle surrendered and allowed the entrance. Jesse's eyes rolled back as Rick's penis penetrated inch by inch until he was sitting on the forest officer's bull balls. Jesse looked out the windshield at a forest road pitted and potholed like the craters of the moon.

"Ok, Ian. Let's go. Take off up this hill. Keep it at 30 or so."

And with that, the engine roared forward and rumbled up the rough road like an elephant. With every bang and bump, Rick's cock drove deeper and deeper into Jesse's stretched hole. Jesse felt the massive meat plow against his virgin prostate that Brandon's shorter cock had never slammed against. It sent shivers of pain and pleasure through his body. Jesse turned his head and saw Brandon with clinched teeth ride Bayard's ample cock, every pothole driving Bayard's penis further into the small firefighter's wrecked hole. The engine rocked and rolled through the potholes and Jesse moaned, gripping his cock, He felt his insides contract and grip Rick's cock like a vise, as rope after rope of hot semen blasted out of Jesse's rigid penis, coating the dashboard and windshield with his nutt with a loud shudder of pleasure.

"Oh God, I'm gonna cum," Bayard shouted.

"Fuck me, I'm cumming," Brandon yelled at almost the same moment. The small firefighter's penis erupted over the front seat, shooting a thick load of sperm onto the side of Ian's face and Rick's red mustache.

Jesse felt Rick grip his waist even tighter and bear down, pushing even harder inside his ruined hole. The thick member swelled and began to give up its seed in a torrent as the man yelled, "Holy Mother of God" and hit the ceiling of the truck with his fist. Jesse could feel the semen leak out of his stretched hole and down his furry legs. Ian brought the engine to a halt on the top of another landing overlooking a large clearcut. He reached down and gripped his dick and pumped it up and down.

"Man, this is killing me, watching you guys," Ian said groaning and jacking.

Rick unceremoniously pulled out of Jesse and pushed him to the middle of the front seat. "Ok, switch, Rookies. Brandon, up front. Jesse, you get in the back. Ian, crawl over here," he said gripping his cock that was already hard again. Ian opened the door and scrambled naked around the front of the engine while a naked Jesse ran around the opposite way, fat dicks flopping back and forth as they ran. Jesse grabbed the handle, his furry legs spread wide to display his large sack and still-hard cock as he jumped in the back with Bayard. Brandon had scrambled over and maneuvered himself into the driver's seat, his penis still leaking a short rope of pearly semen. Jesse started to straddle Bayard's hairy legs to sit on his rigid pole when the older man stopped him.

"Think I'll take a ride on that big boy of yours, Rook," Bayard said, climbing up to sit on Jesse's lap. But he stopped and turned to suck the young guy's cock with loud, sloppy slurps bringing it back to full erection. Rick pushed Ian forward toward the windshield, spreading his meaty ass cheeks apart and licking his dusty rose, probing deep with his tongue until his red mustache and goatee were buried in the blond fuzzy crack. Rick ate like a starving bear, gulping and lapping at Ian's almost-virgin hole, pulling it open and drilling inside while the young guy's face was pressed against the glass in ecstasy. Bayard followed suit and positioned his hairy round mounds against Jesse's face who gripped the husky man's butt and munched deep and hungrily on his hole. Brandon watched the couples engaged in the butt munching and found his penis was rock hard again as well and he longed to have a cock wedged in his ass or his planted in a tight hole as well.

Rick pulled his face out of Ian's ass and coated his rigid pole with another generous dollop of lube, sliding two greasy fingers into the boy's moist hole as Ian groaned. He threw the bottle over the seat. Jesse caught it and he lubed his penis and probed Bayard's manhole with his lubed thumb, feeling the man's ring grip it tightly. Jesse held his cock still and Bayard lowered his ass down on the erection until he was sitting on the rookie's full sack. Up in the front, Ian grunted loudly as Rick's prodigious member impaled him inch by inch.

"Fuck, you're tight, Rookie. How did Ole Tom get up in this hole last night?" Rick said sweating, slowly probing deeper into Ian's anus.

"Bet he shared one of those awesome cookies of his, the ones with the really great weed that make you want to fuck so much," Bayard whispered from the back seat, his words punctuated with grunts as Jesse's cock moved in and out of his hole.

"That true, Rook?" Rick asked with a growl, his penis halfway inside the probie, slow gentle pushes working his tight chute open.

"Yeah, once I ate that thing and he started messing with me, I just wanted him to keep going," Ian groaned. "Fuck, your cock is so huge."

"That's what I like to hear," Rick said. "Ok, Brandon, let's go. Back down the road. Try and hit every bump."

Brandon cranked the engine and disengaged the air break and started down the steep grade. He watched peripherally and saw Rick's cock disappear deeper and deeper into Ian's big butt. Ian groaned and Brandon found a nice washboard section of road and rolled through it at a good speed. The rhythmic bouncing of the engine drove Rick's huge penis further inside his tight hole, bumping hard against his virgin prostate. Ian's cock was leaking copious amounts of precum, a puddle of clear nut honey pooling on the floor mat, a long thin thread stretching from his erection to the floor, glistening in the sun. The engine found a new section of potholes and began to slam up and down hard.

"Mother fuck a duck," Bayard hissed as he rode Jesse's thick cock. He gripped the back of the front seat, his legs spread wide, letting

Jesse's penis piston up and down his ass chute with abandon. Jesse's eyes were closed as he felt his shaft massaged by Bayard's soft anal cavity, rolling his balls back and forth. Jesse could feel his cock bouncing hard against the spongy insides of Bayard's prostate, tapping out a steady beat of desire on the big man's sweet spot.

"I'm gonna shoot," Jesse said feeling his ass contract and send a thick blast of semen deep inside Bayard's manhole.

"Blast off!" Brandon shouted as he neared the bottom of the road and pulled off on a turnout in a cloud of dust. He looked over and Rick was pumping deep and fast into Ian's ass, his legs pulled up resting on the dashboard.

"Jesus!" Ian yelled as his cock exploded in creamy goodness all over his belly, dripping down on his rigid pole to his fat sack, clinging to the furry blond curls in his pubic bush. He fell back against Rick who was still deep inside his hole. Rick gripped the boy's nipples and pinched them softly, nibbling the side of his face with his lips. Ian complained as the fat cock was pulled from his spent anus.

"Oh god, you ruined my bobbum," he barked while the rest of guys laughed.

"That's right, Probie. Your equipmunk is mine!" Rich snapped. It was clear all of them watched "The League" and knew about Bobbum Man.

"Get over here Bran," Rick ordered. "I haven't had my second nut yet and your ass needs filling. Ian, climb into the back with Bayard. Jesse, start driving."

Moments later, the engine was rocking back up the rutted road as Rick's cock was pile driven again and again into Brandon's ass. His furry hole was like a chestnut wreath circling Rick's girth, the furry cheeks sitting on the forest officer's fat nutsack, rolling the plums around in the bag. Jesse looked in the back and saw Bayard and Ian in a 69 position, sucking long and hard on each other's cocks. Brandon faced Rick, gripping the man's shoulders as he rode the big pole up the rough road. When Jesse hit the washboard section again, the constant hard banging sent Brandon over the edge and his dick shot thick semen up Rick's chest to his chin, gluing the men together. Brandon found Rick's mouth and kissed him, feeling his tongue play with his boss who tasted of sweat and sex. Rick grunted loudly and unloaded his orgasm into Brandon's anus, with three hard blasts. As Jesse pulled up on the remote landing again, Rick's penis slipped out of the rookie's hole with a soft plop. A small stream of white spilled out and joined the pool of Ian's precum already decorating the floor mat.

"Now that's what I'm fucking talking about. Been a long time since we had rookies this promising," Rick said breathlessly. The rest of the guys sat back and caught their breath. The cab of the engine was a funk of sperm, sweat, and ass. Rick slapped Brandon on the butt and slid him off his lap and back on the seat.

"Too bad we can't fight fire like this all this time, but might get a little warm on our bare ass," Brandon quipped.

"I hear you, probie. OK men, grab your pants and come with me. Want to show you something before we head back," Rick ordered.

The mostly-naked rookies grabbed their gear and followed Rick and Bayard, who were still pulling their pants back up as they headed off the landing into a nearby thick swath of forest. The men found a faint path thick with ferns, salal, and coastal huckleberry, and followed it deeper and deeper into the woods. The large Douglas Fir and alder trees muffled their footsteps as they hiked further.

Jesse smiled, feeling his dick and sack bounce around, enjoying the warm summer air caressing his furry legs. This is the weirdest shit I have ever done in my life, he thought. But something else was there too. This growing loyalty and sense of belonging. And for the love of God, he thought, who would have known all these guys were cock crazy too? Some were young and some were older. Some were married and yet still seemed to crave cock. Some were divorced, some single, some virgin, some veteran. He searched back through all the memories of conversations he had with his father, all the times he had accompanied him to the unit office. Was there a clue about all this back then and he was just too young to see it? He did remember back when he was a boy, ten or maybe younger, he would hang out in the locker room area with his dad and saw plenty of the fire crew coming in and out of the showers. He had loved that, seeing all the different shapes and sizes of bodies. That experience alone had answered most of his questions about puberty and what happened to your body when you grew up. He had seen all that long before he had started taking showers in junior high and high school. All the men had been friendly with each other and clearly comfortable being naked together, but he didn't remember it seeming odd or intimate in a different way.

He remembered that time when he had come home unexpectedly from school due to feeling sick. He lived close enough to the school to walk and the school had contacted his mom. She told him to walk home since his dad was on his day off. He must have been twelve or thirteen. He remembered getting home and seeing another truck in the driveway. He had dropped his backpack in the kitchen and grabbed some orange juice. He heard a noise from upstairs and went up to see his dad. Right before he opened his parents' bedroom door, he heard a noise from within. He waited a moment listening to the voices: his dad's and another man's. They were laughing quietly and shushing one another, hurrying around in the room. Jesse quietly opened the door a small crack and saw his dad and the other man, Joey Goldman from the fire crew, quickly dressing. Both were mostly naked and were searching around for the rest of their clothes. As Joey moved around the bed and bent down to grab his socks, Jesse watched his dad walk up closely behind him, stopping against Joey's back. Jesse didn't know what that was all about back then, but now it all began to make sense. He had quietly closed the door and made his way to his own room.

The fire crew pushed through a last sharp curve on the trail and came to a small clearing. A rock face of a cliff was in front of them, wet with a constant curtain of water dripping and flowing down the moss covered sides. The rock face ended in a pool about twelve feet across, steam gently rising off the surface. Water on the far side of the pool flowed out in a small stream that chattered over stones in a shallow rivulet down the steep slope that dropped away from the pool on the far side. The firefighters gathered around the pool.

There was a rustling behind the crew. The guys turned their heads and saw the other crew members making their way into the clearing. Jordan, Nick, and Aaron walked in naked wearing only their boots. They were followed by Eric, Chad, Sam, Ben, Colton, Tom, and Jake. The men closed ranks and stood shoulder to shoulder around the pool.

"Welcome to Patterson Hot Springs. This is a sacred place for Hart Mountain Hotshots. For many years, we have brought rookies here for a welcome initiation to our brotherhood. This place is named for one of our fallen brothers, Jason Patterson, Jesse's dad. Jason Patterson was Squad boss and the clear leader of our crew for years," Jake spoke in an eloquent soft, husky voice. "We bring our new rookies here to bathe after we breed them and make them part of our brotherhood. Just like we joined together with you with our cocks, we join together with you in our commitment to serve together, to protect natural resources as best we can, and to keep each other safe. Together, we bathe away our separations and individuality and become a true crew. So brothers, let's wash and celebrate our new crew members."

With that, Jake began to unbutton his shirt. He bent to unlace his boots. The others began to follow suit. The rookies quickly removed their boots. Brandon noticed when Jordan bent over to unlace his boots, the black hairs around his asshole were matted with lube and spunk. He looked over at Jesse who obviously saw the same evidence. The look of acknowledgement reflected on both their faces. More than one engine crew had been pounded today from the looks of it.

Jake stood naked on the side of the pool, his heavy penis resting on large nuts in a closely trimmed sack. He stepped down into the water. The other veteran members of the crew were now naked as well, and stepped in behind him. The rookies joined in next, settling in between the older crew members into the hot, steamy spring.

They soaked in the water up to their necks, floating in the hot water. Big furry feet touched in the center of the pool. Jesse felt Colton's hand slide around his penis and stroke him until he was hard. On the other side, He reached over and gripped Eric's cock and stroked him as well. It appeared all the crew was fondling one another as they talked and laughed about the day's driving training. From the sound of it, all of the engines were going to need plenty of cleaning to remove the buckets of sperm that apparently had flowed all over the vehicles.

Jesse looked around at these men, young and older and felt his heart swell. He was filled with emotion, his ass was tired, and he felt at home. That part of his heart that he had missed since his dad had died felt a little bit fuller. He laid his head back and enjoyed the hot water and the hands gripping his cock.

Later that night, after dinner and another clean up in the showers, Jesse spent a nice slow time eating Brandon's ass before sliding his length deep within his buddy's pussy. Brandon's rectal walls gripped Jesse's shaft holding him deep within him. Brandon's hairy legs wrapped around Jesse's waist, pulling him deeper inside. The firefighters kissed long and slow, tasting each other. Jesse's scratchy chin whiskers rubbed against Brandon's smooth skin, returning back to his friend's lips and kissing again.

As he felt his orgasm quicken, Jesse pulled out and aimed his penis at Brandon's open mouth and unloaded his balls with thick white semen spurting on his buddy's lips, tongue, and mouth. Brandon stroked his cock and fired his own load onto his hairy belly. Jesse bent down and kissed his friend, tasting his seed on his lips. He lay back on the pillows and Brandon's curly head lay on his arm. They lay listening to crickets and the wind and Tom and Ian's noisy lovemaking on one side and Ben and Colton's on the other.

"Quite a day we had, huh, Frodo?"

"Sure did, Sam. What do you think about all this cocksucking and fucking?"

"Well, I can't say I expected all this. But I don't know, somehow I'm not surprised either. Just seems right. Sure feels right," Jesse answered. "By the way, why the hell did you take that Fleshlight in your fire pack?"

Brandon started laughing and Jesse joined in. They laughed until tears ran down their cheeks and someone from another tent shouted, "Shut the fuck up!" Then they muffled their renewed laughs in their pillows. Brandon's hand rubbed on Jesse's chest, playing with the curly chest hair and his brown nipples.

"I'm just glad we are in the fellowship together, Sam. I love you, you know."

"Yeah, I know, Numbnuts. Love you too."

TO BE CONTINUED...

Here is a sample from another story you may enjoy:

ANGUS MACGREGOR

SOUTH PATROL POUNDING

Gay Romance Series

Hart Mountain Hotshots Book 4

THEY HAD fallen into a quiet little pattern that was both endearing to Ben and more than a little annoying. They had been together now for two years, two huge years. So much had happened it was hard to think of it all. They were now a couple, and that was good. But it was also a slippery slope, Ben thought. Maybe a bit too safe and predictable. Even that enjoyable butt munch in the shower was somehow expected now. But that kind of thinking made Ben feel like an asshole. He knew how lucky he was and how much more sex he and Colton had than most of the other married guys on the crew.

The guys on the crew routinely pumped both of them for details on their sex life, which was fun to share in small bits now and then and hear the complaints from the men who were getting very little sex at home. Some of the other married guys, if they were to be believed, seemed to fuck as much as Ben and Colton did. And yet, they still seemed to have plenty of interest and energy to connect with the other guys on the crew from time to time.

The guys jumped into their Dodge Ram pickup and took off toward the crew compound at the district office. The morning was bright and clear, dry with a bit of an east wind that could cause them all some trouble later on that afternoon. The rookies were finished with fire school and were beginning to go along on regular patrols in the afternoon looking for smoke, and general compound maintenance.

"So which of these idiot rookies do we get today?" Colton asked, sliding on his sunglasses.

His muscled arms were covered with a solid dusting of blond fur. The tank top he wore was fitted tight to his husky, muscled frame. His blond armpit fur blew in the wind as he rolled down the window. He reached over and gripped Ben's large hand and laced his fingers into the man's grip.

Ben smiled and squeezed the fingers tightly. God! Why does this simple touch still get his blood racing, he wondered, remembering the first time Colton had held his hand.

"I think we get Jesse and Frodo," Ben said as Colton ran his finger over the band on his ring finger. Ben noticed he did that all the time.

"Tricksy Hobbitses," Colton said in his best Gollum voice. "I stroked Jesse's cock the other day when we were in the hot spring pool."

"Oh you did," Ben said with a fake offended voice. "So how was that?"

"Kid's gotta nice dick," Colton said with a grin. "What about you, did you get to check out the hobbit?"

"He's got a great ass," Ben said.

"Did you bring Tom and Jerry?"

"Yep, they are in the gear bag. Lube too."

Colton pushed the gas down and the engine roared to life. "Gonna be a great day, sweetheart."

"SHIT, HAVE you seen my socks?" Brandon asked in exasperation, looking under the bed for the third time.

Jess pulled his t-shirt over his head. "No, I told you just take a pair of mine," Jesse said back.

The guys continued to rush around to get dressed. Ever since Brandon had moved into Jesse's room, mornings had been chaos since neither of them were all that organized. Jesse's mom had been supportive of Brandon moving in, feeling it would help Jesse feel more settled or something. She had not questioned the boys sharing his room and the one bed.

Richie, Jesse's younger brother, had taken to Brandon like a new puppy, laughing at his jokes and hanging on him all the time. Jesse had noticed the little guy making sure to sit by Brandon on the couch when they were watching television or at dinner, clearly eager for Brandon's attention. He thought it was cool though a bit sad since the little twerp used to do that with him.

Probably the hardest thing about sharing a room in the house with his brother and mom was the fact that he and Brandon had to be so quiet at night when they had sex. In fact, most nights they waited long after they stopped hearing noises from any of the other rooms before continuing their newly found hobby of fucking night and day. Half the time, they were pressing their faces into pillows to stifle the moans and shouts of pleasure as they took turns pumping as much semen as possible into each other's ass.

The kissing and sucking just kept getting better and better, Jesse thought. He wondered how long it would be before he simply had to tell his mom the truth: her little boy was queer and he loved it. Brandon seemed to feel the same, though he was relieved not to be at home with his parents having to disguise all interesting sounds from the bedroom.

The guys rushed out of the house and piled in Jesse's truck and took off to the district office. Jesse clicked on the iPod and blasted Jason Aldean's "Night Train" all the way to work. The morning air was already warm, flowing in the windows. It ruffled through the tight curls on Brandon's hair and Jesse reached over and ran his fingers through them.

"Love you, Frodo," Jesse said with a grin.

"Back at you, Dildo," Brandon said, stretching over and planting a big wet kiss on the scruff of Jesse's unshaved cheek.

The guys roared into the parking lot about thirty seconds before needing to clock in. They dropped their packs in the locker room and rushed to the time clock, jockeying with each other to get their card in the clock before it was too late.

"Yessss," Brandon hissed looking at his card reading 0900.

Jesse punched immediately after him and looked at his card in disgust. "Goddamn it," he whispered holding up the card for Brandon to see. It read 0901.

"Dude you were totally screwed," Brandon said with a wicked smile.

"Yeah well fuck you, asshole," Jesse snarled back in a whisper. "You'll pay for that later."

Ben walked up and motioned for Jesse and Brandon to come over to the side of the shop so he could talk to them. Brandon couldn't help but stare again at the thick mat of black fur that carpeted Ben's arms and neck. Even the tops of his fingers were blanketed in thick black fur, which made his olive skin look even darker. His day growth of beard was thick and stubbly, fuller than a full week of growth for Jesse or Brandon.

"Okay, ladies. You will be riding with us today. As part of your continued initiation into Hart Mountain Hotshots, Colton and I have a tradition of our own." Ben reached into the cargo pockets in his pants and brought out two shining black butt plugs. They were about four inches long, cone shaped stoppers that started in a small rounded tip and flared to a wide midsection, then ended in a narrow neck and flat base. Jesse and Brandon's eyes popped wide open as they stared at the plugs.

"Gonna need you to go slide these babies up your cooters," Ben said with a wicked grin. "You need to keep them up there while you work today. All day. No matter what, don't take them out unless you ask us first. Got it?"

Both rookies gulped and tentatively took the hard rubber plug and looked around to see if others were watching. Ben tossed a tube of lube at Brandon and gave him a wink.

"Lickety split, boys. We got a full day of work to do," Ben said…

If you enjoyed this sample then look for **Hart Mountain Hotshots Book 4: South Patrol Pounding.**

Also by this Author

The Hotshot Brotherhood

Brokeback Buddies

From the Author

If you enjoyed any of my books then please share the love and click like on my books in Amazon.

If you write me a review and send me an email I will send you a free book, or many.
(Just know that these emails are filtered by my publisher.)

Good news is always welcome.

One Last Thing, For Kindle Readers...

When you turn the page, Kindle will give you the opportunity to rate this book and share your thoughts on Facebook and Twitter. If you enjoyed my writings, would you please take a few seconds to let your friends know about it? Because... when they enjoy they will be grateful to you and so will I.

Thank You!

Angus MacGregor
angus_macgregor@awesomeauthors.org